My First
RIDDLES

Pictures by Corwin

HarperFestival®
A Division of HarperCollinsPublishers

Text copyright © 1998 by HarperCollins Publishers Inc. Illustrations copyright © 1998 by Judith Hoffman Corwin.
HarperCollins®, ≝®, HarperFestival®, and Harper Growing Tree and logo are trademarks of HarperCollins Publishers Inc. Printed in the U.S.A. All rights reserved.
Library of Congress catalog card number: 97-73144   http://www.harperchildrens.com   Design by Tom Starace

For Jules Arthur and Oliver Jamie

What wakes you up
at the beginning
of the day?

It's bright, round,
and yellow—
at night it
goes away.

sun

MILK

What has fur,
a tail,
whiskers,
and claws?

It likes to catch mice
with its four
little paws.

cat

What has a ladder
and hose
and a flashing
red light?

It zooms to
the rescue,
day or night.

fire truck

Who has
a carrot nose,
and is cold
and round?

If the sun comes out,
he'll melt
to the ground.

snowman

What has wrinkly skin
and a very
long nose?

It carries its trunk
wherever
it goes.

elephant

What do you wear
when rain falls
from the sky?

It has buttons
and pockets,
and helps
keep you dry.

raincoat

Who's near you
all day
and beside you
at night?

He's cute,
soft, and furry–
when you're scared,
hold him tight!

teddy bear

Who is yellow
and floats and
has a bright orange
beak?

He's a friend
in the tub,
squeeze him—
he'll squeak.

rubber duck

You're my PLAYMATE for always,
and my JOY ever after.

Hanging out WITH YOU
is where I want to be...
eating ice cream sundaes
or watching the TV.

UNDER your umbrella,
behind you on a bike.
BY you and BESIDE you
is what I REALLY like.

"Do you love me just AS MUCH
   when I'm FAR away from home?
Is your loving still THE SAME
   in distant lands I roam?"

I love you NEAR or FAR.

I love you HIGH or LOW.

My love is there with you

WHEREVER you may go.

Camp

"Even when I'm SICK...
    and I can't get out of bed?
Do you love me better HEALTHY
    than with fever in my head?"

I love you sick or able.
You're ALWAYS you to me,
the ONE I LOVE forevermore.
Undeniably.

I CAN'T IMAGINE life
before YOU came along...
me there singing senseless,
no MEANING to my song.

Call it MEANT TO BE
or simply blessed fate,
you fill my heart WITH LOVE...
and for THAT I celebrate.

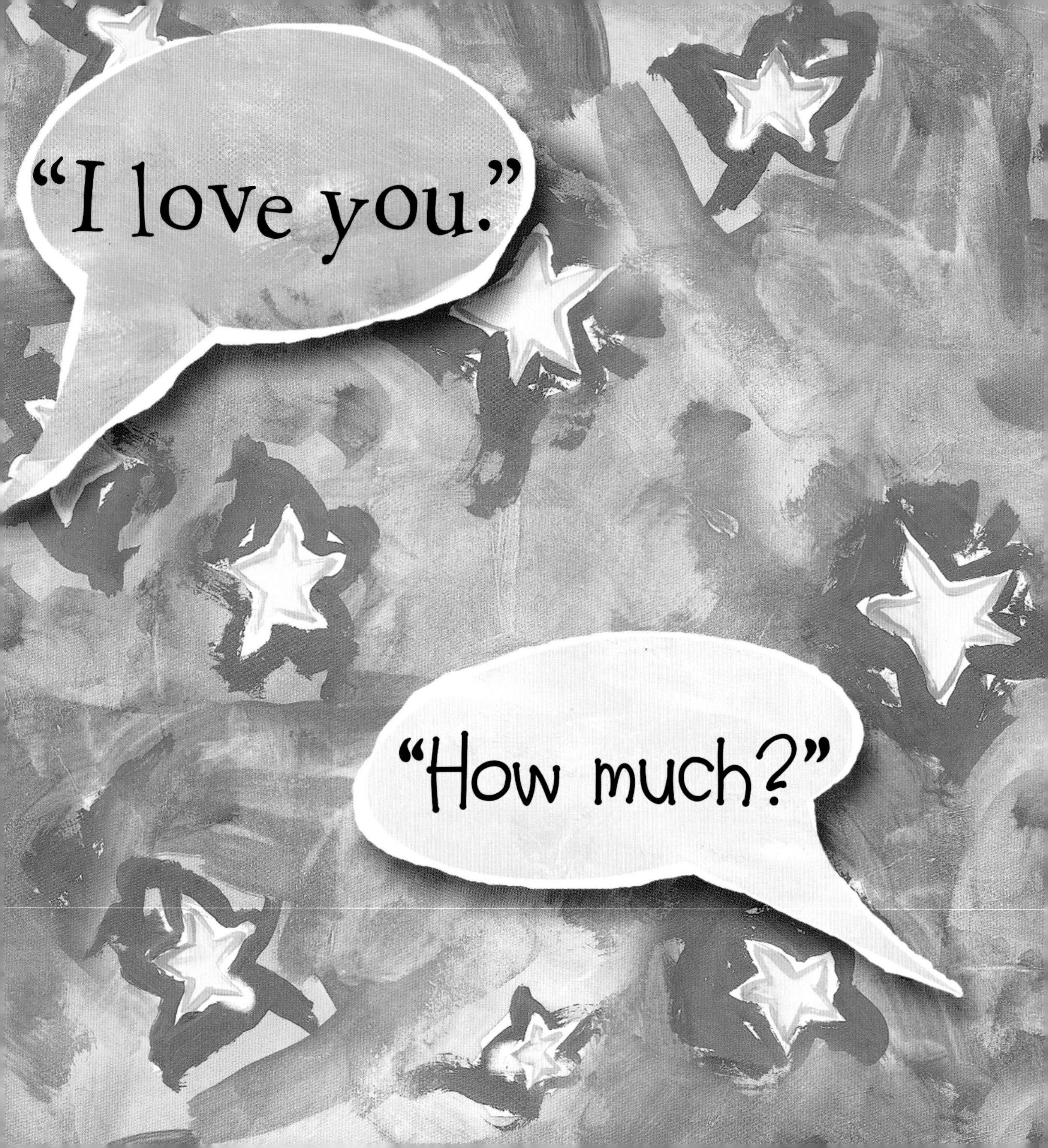
"I love you."
"How much?"

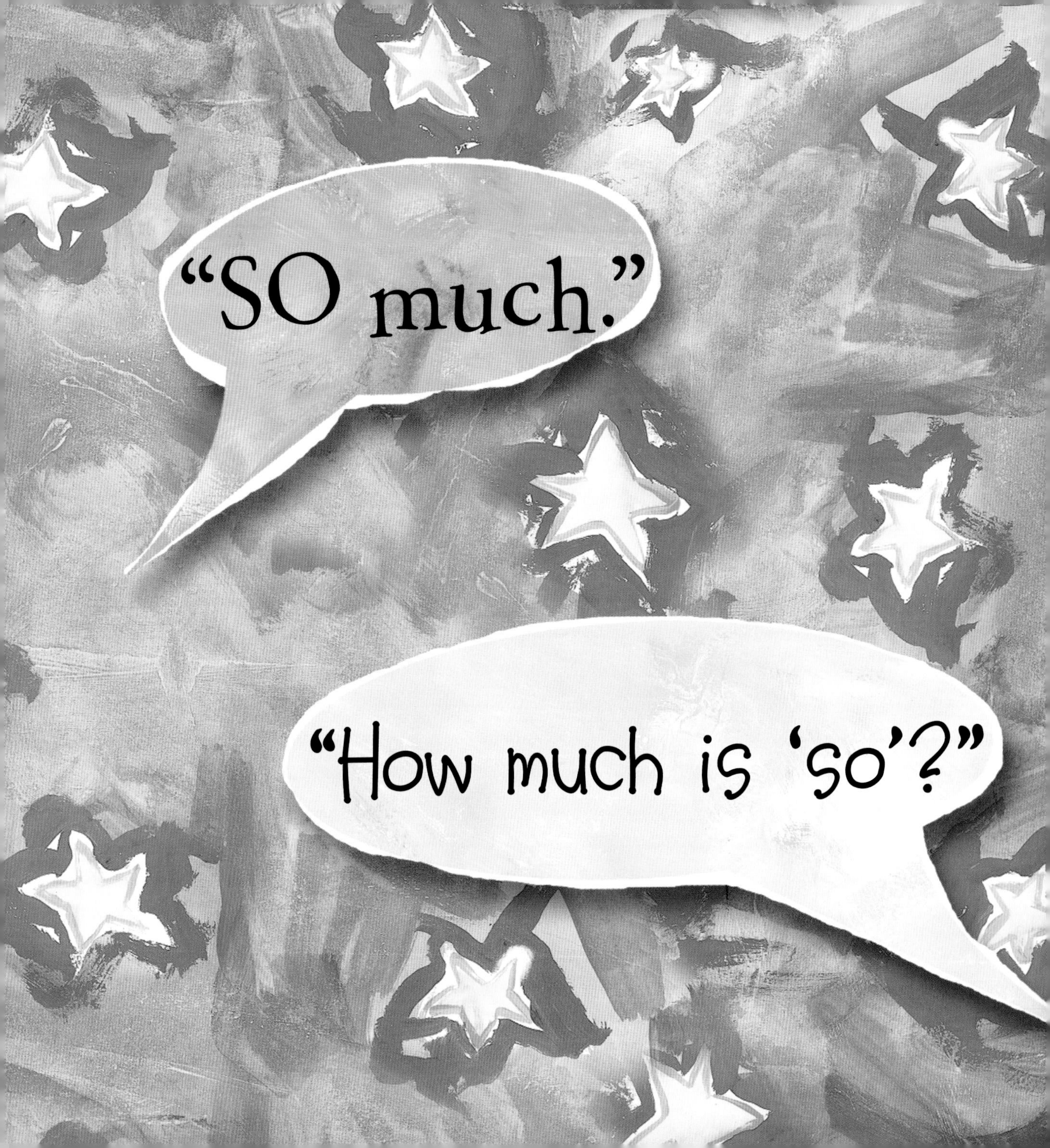
"SO much."
"How much is 'so'?"